MW00444616

Ludwig van
BEETHOVEN

TRIO No. 3

Op. 1, No. 3
in C Minor

FOR PIANO, VIOLIN AND CELLO

K 09709

Kalmus

Drittes Trio.

Dem Fürsten Carl von Lichnowsky gewidmet.

Op. 1. No 3.

BELWIN MILLS PUBLISHING CORP.

PRINTED IN U.S.A.

Andante cantabile con Variázioni.

Andante cantabile con Variazioni.

Var. I.

Ludwig van

BEETHOVEN

TRIO No. 3

Op. 1, No. 3
in C Minor

VIOLIN

K 09709

TRIO III.

Op. 1. Nº 3.

Adagio. Tempo I.

Andante cantabile con Variazioni.

Var. I.

Var. II.

A *Kalmus Classic Edition*

Ludwig van

BEETHOVEN

TRIO No. 3

Op. 1, No. 3
in C Minor

CELLO

K 09709

Kalmus

TRIO III.

Op. 1. No 3.

BELWIN MILLS PUBLISHING CORP.

PRINTED IN U.S.A.

VIOLONCELLO.

VIOLONCELLO.

Trio.